POLE

ARCTIC OCEAN

EUROPE

ASIA

MIDDLE
EAST

China

AFRICA

India

INDIAN OCEAN

Sumatra
Borneo

N

W                E

S

ANTARCTICA

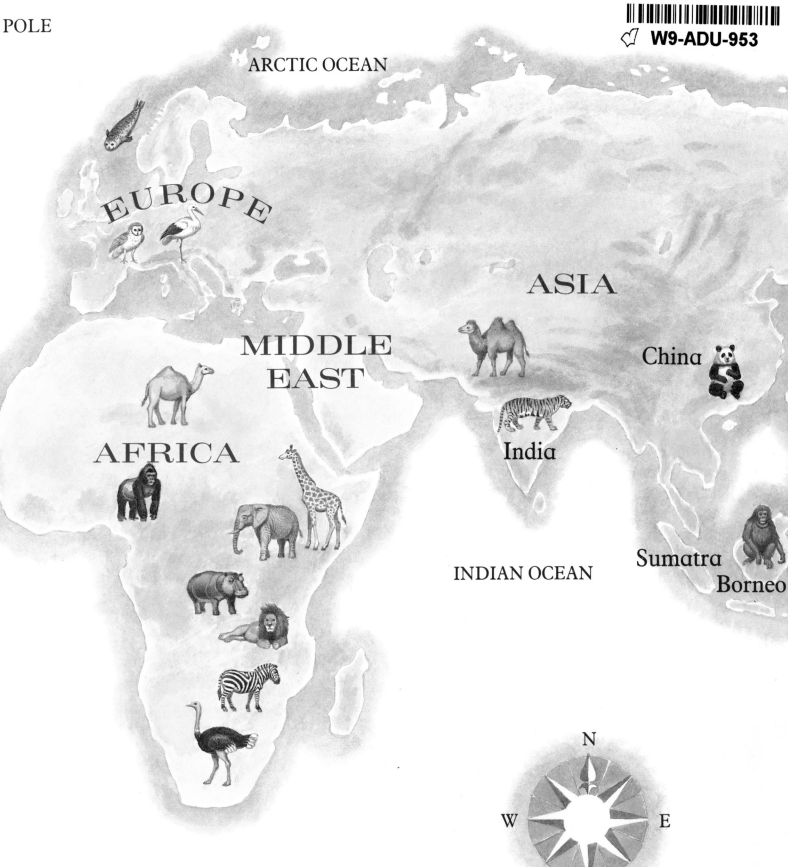

# MY FIRST BOOK OF ANIMALS

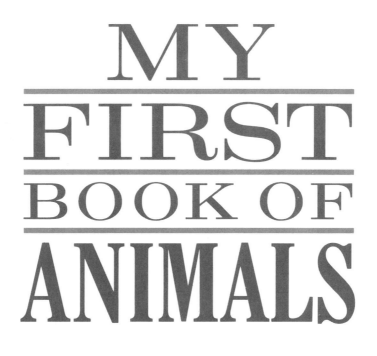

BY
## JENNY WOOD

ILLUSTRATED BY
## PETER BARRETT AND
## JOHN BUTLER

**WARNER
JUVENILE
BOOKS**

A Warner Communications Company
New York

# THIS BOOK BELONGS TO

*Design:* David Bennett

*Editor:* Ruth Thomson

*Consultant:* Julian Hector
*Zoologist and Broadcaster*

Warner Juvenile Books Edition
First American Edition
Copyright © 1989 Conran Octopus Limited
All rights reserved.

This Warner Juvenile Books edition is published by
arrangement with Conran Octopus Limited, London.

Warner Books, Inc., 666 Fifth Avenue, New York, NY 10103
A Warner Communications Company
Printed in Italy
First Warner Juvenile Books Printing: October 1989

10 9 8 7 6 5 4 3 2 1

**Library of Congress Cataloging-in-Publication Data**

Wood, Jenny.
  My first book of animals / Jenny Wood; illustrated by Peter
Barrett and John Butler — Warner Juvenile Books ed.
  p. cm.

  Summary: Brief text and illustrations introduce the habits and
habitats of a variety of animals.
  ISBN: 1-55782-330-8
  1. Animals — Miscellanea — Juvenile literature. [1. Animals]
I. Barrett, P.J.H., ill. II. Butler, John, ill. III. Title
QL49.W868 1989
598 — dc20                                    89 — 14606
                                                  CIP
                                                  AC

# CONTENTS

# LIONS

Lions are big cats. They are found in Africa. They live in groups called prides.

Each pride is made up of one or two male lions, several females, and their young.

Lions like to rest during the heat of the day.

Lion cubs learn how to hunt by chasing their mother's tail and fighting with each other.

Lions can go without food
for several days, but they need
to drink a lot of water.

In the mornings and in the evenings,
when it is cool, the lionesses
hunt for food. The male lions
stay behind with the cubs.

5

# BIG CATS

These animals are big cats, too. They live
in hot countries in different parts of
the world.

The cheetah can run faster than any other animal
on land. But when it runs at top speed it tires
quickly because it uses up so much energy.

Can you see the tiger
in the long grass?
Its stripes help it to hide
from other animals.

A leopard often lies along the branch of a tree, enjoying the shade. Sometimes it drags its food up into the tree to eat.

Jaguars are very good swimmers. They live on riverbanks in the rain forests of South America. They like to eat fish and other small creatures from the river.

# ELEPHANTS

Elephants are the biggest of all the animals that live on land. They are found in Africa and Asia. Asian elephants have smaller ears and shorter tusks, as well as much smaller bodies.

African Elephants

Elephants live in groups called herds so that they can protect their young from danger.

Asian Elephant

In India, people use elephants to help them with heavy work.

Young elephants like to touch and stroke each other with their trunks. Sometimes they pretend to fight.

Elephants like to keep clean. They use their trunks to squirt water all over their bodies. The water also keeps them cool.

# BIG BIRDS

## OSTRICH

Ostriches are the world's largest living birds. They are found on the hot, dry grasslands of central Africa. Ostriches cannot fly, but they can run very fast.

When ostrich chicks are in danger, they often lie flat on the ground and pretend to be dead!

## EMU

Emus are a little smaller than ostriches. They are found only in Australia. Like ostriches, emus cannot fly, but they can run fast and swim well. They eat fruit, plants, and insects.

Emu chicks have lovely black and yellow stripes.

# WHITE STORK

White storks are found in Europe, Africa, and Asia. They often build their nests on the roofs of houses and are thought to bring good luck.

# LESSER FLAMINGO

Lesser flamingos are found beside the lakes of East Africa. They live in large groups called colonies.

Flamingos sleep and rest standing on one leg.

Slits inside the top part of a flamingo's bill help the bird strain the water and mud for the tiny plants and insects it likes to eat.

# HIPPOPOTAMUSES

Hippos are found in the rivers and lakes of Africa.
They live in groups called herds.
Hippos eat grass and other plants. At night,
they come out of the water to look for food.

If hippos stay out in the hot sun
for too long, their skin becomes cracked
and sore. Swimming in the mud or water
helps keep their skin soft.

Mud also keeps hippos
cool in hot weather.

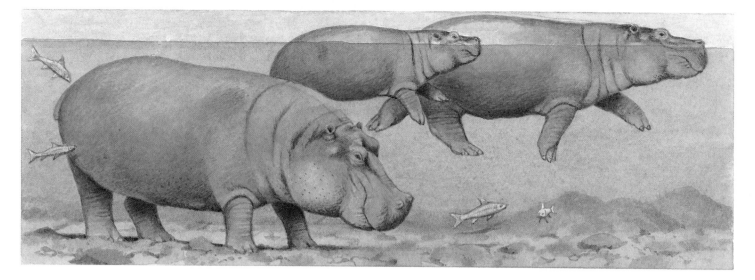

Sometimes a hippo will take a deep breath and then dive right underwater. It can hold its breath for about six minutes while it walks along the riverbed.

Baby hippos are born underwater. They are soon taught to swim.

When hippos are afraid, they often gather into a circle in the water to protect themselves.

Young hippos love to play together in the water.

A yawn is a sign that a hippo is angry or frightened.

# CROCODILES

Crocodiles and alligators are found in many of the world's hot countries. They are able to live on land and in water.

Little birds fly into a crocodile's mouth and pick out scraps of food from between its teeth. This helps keep the crocodile's mouth clean and healthy.

Female crocodiles and alligators both lay eggs. As soon as baby crocodiles have hatched, their mother carries them in her mouth to a safe place at the water's edge.

The babies stay in this nursery area for several months. They learn how to swim and how to catch food.

# ALLIGATORS

Animals have to be very careful when they come to the water to drink in case an alligator or crocodile tries to catch them.

Crocodiles and alligators seem very similar. But if you look carefully, you will see that their heads are different shapes. An alligator's head is short and square, and a crocodile's is long and narrow.

Their teeth are different too. When an alligator's mouth is shut, you can see only its upper teeth. A crocodile shows some of its lower teeth as well.

# POLAR BEARS

Polar bears are found on the ice around the cold Arctic Ocean. They live alone and spend most of their time hunting for food. They have thick, furry soles on their feet to help them walk on the ice.

Cubs stay with their mother for one or two years. She teaches them how to look after themselves.

Cubs are born in the winter in a special den that their mother digs under the ice.

Polar bears are good swimmers. When a polar bear comes out of the icy water, it quickly shakes itself dry so that its fur doesn't freeze.

Polar bears feed on seals. They wait beside the breathing hole the seal has made in the ice until it comes up for air.

# SEALS

There are many different kinds of seals. Most of them live in the cold seas near the North and South Poles. Some seals have a layer of fat called blubber under their skin that keeps them warm in the cold water. Others have thick fur.

Baby seals are called pups. They stay with their mother until they are able to catch fish for themselves.

Seals are very good swimmers. They move through the water by using their powerful front flippers and by moving their bodies up and down.

Seals come up to the surface of the water to breathe. This Weddell seal has found a breathing hole in the ice.

Sometimes a seal sleeps in the water with its body straight up and down and only its head above the surface.

18

# WALRUSES

Walruses live near the North Pole. They spend a lot of time on land as well as in the water. They live in groups called herds, and hundreds of them can be seen together on rocky beaches.

A walrus has a mustache of stiff whiskers, which helps guide food into its mouth. Walruses eat clams, mussels, starfish, and shrimp.

A young walrus is called a calf. It stays with its mother until it's about two years old.

Male walruses have two very long teeth called tusks. They use them to dig for food on the sea bottom.

19

# JUNGLE BIRDS

These brightly colored birds
live in the rain forests
of South America.

The toucan's long
bill has ridged
edges for tearing
up food. It tosses
its head back
so that the food
falls down its
throat.

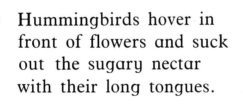

Hummingbirds hover in
front of flowers and suck
out the sugary nectar
with their long tongues.

This yellow-headed parrot looks for food in the treetops. It eats fruit, nuts, seeds, and berries.

Toucans live in lush, dense treetops, where there are few open spaces for them to fly.

Scarlet macaws usually fly in pairs. They travel so close together that their wings almost touch.

# MONKEYS

Monkeys are found in many different parts of the world.
Most monkeys live in trees, but some live on the ground.
They eat fruit, nuts, plants, and insects.

When it is small, a baby monkey is carried on its mother's stomach. When it grows older, it travels on her back.

Mandrills live in Africa. The adult male mandrill is the largest of all monkeys. The bright colors on its face frighten away animals which might attack it.

These South American spider monkeys can hang from tree branches by their tails!

This mother baboon is combing her baby's fur with her fingers to get rid of bits of dry skin and insects.

Baboons are found in Africa. They live mainly on the ground. Young baboons love to play games.

# KANGAROOS

Wild kangaroos live only in Australia.
They hop from place to place, using their
strong back legs to push themselves forward.

A baby kangaroo is called a joey. When
it is born, it crawls at once into a
pouch on its mother's stomach. It stays in
the pouch for several months, drinking
its mother's milk.

A kangaroo's tail is almost as long as
the rest of its body. It helps the
animal keep its balance.

Kangaroos eat grass. They can go without
food for several days, but they must
always have water to drink.

Sometimes male kangaroos fight each other. They balance on their tails and try to kick each other with their back legs.

When the weather is hot, kangaroos spend most of the day sleeping in the shade. But at least one kangaroo always stays awake, on guard.

# SNAKES

Most snakes live in hot countries. A few are poisonous and dangerous to people. Snakes move by wiggling along the ground.

Some snakes can hide easily because the color and pattern of their skin matches their surroundings.

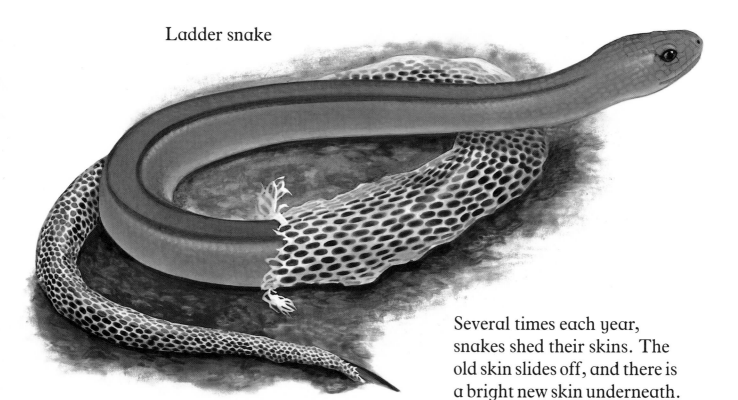

Bushmaster

Ladder snake

Several times each year, snakes shed their skins. The old skin slides off, and there is a bright new skin underneath.

Some snakes kill by twisting their bodies tightly around their prey. These snakes are called constrictors.

Emerald tree boa constrictor

All snakes have long, forked tongues. Some may also have two long, pointed teeth called fangs which they use to kill their prey.

This rattlesnake is one of the most dangerous snakes. When it moves, the end of its tail makes a noise like a rattle.

Rattlesnake

# CORAL REEF

Corals are thousands of tiny, identical animals that live together in a group. They are found in many of the world's warm seas. Some have a hard shell around them and are called hard corals. Others have no shell and are known as soft corals.

Soft corals sway gently in the water.

Hard corals grow into beautiful shapes.

Coral trout

This huge starfish, called the crown of thorns, is the Great Barrier Reef's enemy because it likes to eat corals.

Harlequin tusk fish

Blue starfish

Thousands of brightly colored fish live among the corals. Many of them live in large groups. This helps keep them safe from attack by larger fish or by sharks.

Corals often join together to form a coral reef. Coral reefs grow only in warm, shallow water, where the heat of the sun reaches below the surface. The world's largest coral reef is the famous Great Barrier Reef off the northeast coast of Australia.

Blue angel fish

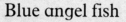

Red fire fish

This clown fish has a secluded hiding place among the tentacles of a sea anemone. Other fish are frightened by the sea anemone's poisonous sting, but the clown fish is protected from the sting by its own body mucus.

# GIANT PANDA

There are probably fewer than two hundred giant pandas living in the wild. They are found only in a small area of China.

Giant pandas spend most of each day eating. Their favorite food is a tough, woody plant called bamboo.

Although giant pandas live on the ground, they will climb trees if they are frightened or want to sleep.

# KOALAS

Koalas are found in Australia. Like giant pandas, koalas are fussy about their food. They eat only the leaves of certain kinds of eucalyptus trees.

Some eucalyptus leaves make koalas sick. Koalas can tell which ones are not good to eat by smelling them.

# BIRDS OF PREY

There are many different kinds of birds of prey. All of them have large eyes, hooked beaks, and strong, sharp claws called talons. They're called "birds of prey" because they catch and eat other birds, furry animals, snakes, fish, and insects.

## GOLDEN EAGLE

The golden eagle is one of the largest birds of prey. It has very wide wings with big feathers at the end to help it soar through the air.

An eagle's nest is called an aerie. The golden eagle builds its nest high up in a tree or on the ledge of a steep cliff. The nest is made from twigs and leaves. Golden eagles return to the same nesting place year after year. Each year, they add more twigs and leaves to their nest.

# BARN OWL

Owls hunt at night. They have very good hearing, and their huge eyes help them see well in the moonlight.

Owls cannot move their eyes at all. If an owl wants to look sideways or behind, it has to move its head. Owls can turn their heads almost full circle - and even upside down.

The soft fringes along the edges of some of an owl's feathers help it to fly almost silently.

Owls call to each other through the night air. Different kinds of owls make different sounds.

# GRIZZLY BEARS

Grizzly bears are found in western Canada and in Alaska, living in forests on the mountain sides. They have shaggy fur, humped shoulders, sharp teeth and long, sharp claws. Male grizzlies are called boars. Female grizzlies are called sows.

Grizzlies usually live alone. Each bear has its own area of land, called a "home range." It leaves scents on the bark of trees all the way around its home range to let other bears know where it lives.

34

Grizzlies have a very good sense of smell.
They will eat almost anything, but they especially
love honey from wild bees' nests. In
summer, they catch fish from the rivers.

Young grizzlies enjoy playing together.
They soon learn to find food for
themselves.

# APES

Gorillas, chimpanzees, orangutans, and gibbons are all apes. They do not have tails. Gorillas like to stay on the ground, but the other apes enjoy climbing high up into the trees.

Chimpanzees like to eat insects called termites, which they catch by poking a twig inside the termites' home.

Chimpanzees live in Africa. They chatter to each other all day long, using their own sounds and signs.

Gorillas are the biggest members of the ape family and are very peaceful, friendly animals. They live in Africa too.

Old male gorillas grow patches of white hair on their backs, and are called "silverbacks."

Orangutans live in the rain forests on the islands of Sumatra and Borneo, in Southeast Asia. They spend most of their time in the trees.

An orangutan sleeps in a nest of small branches that it builds in the fork of a tree. Sometimes it makes a new nest every night.

Gibbons are also found in parts of Southeast Asia. They have very long arms to help them swing easily through the trees.

A male gibbon has a large pouch under his throat. When he calls to another gibbon, the pouch swells up and makes his cry sound even louder. This call is often used as a warning to other gibbon families to stay off his territory.

# CAMELS

Some camels live in the hot deserts of North Africa and the Middle East. These camels have a single hump on their backs. Other camels live in the cold deserts of Asia. They have two humps. Their shaggy coats keep them warm.

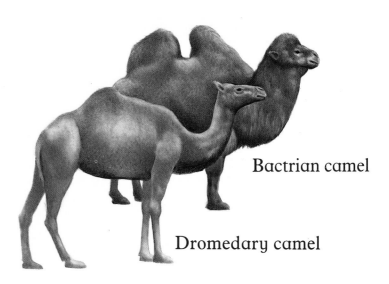

Bactrian camel

Dromedary camel

A camel can store water in its body. One long drink will last for several days.

Camels are used for carrying goods and people. They are sometimes known as "ships of the desert."

Patches of hard skin protect a camel's chest and knees when it kneels down.

A camel's hump contains fat. This gives the animal enough energy to make a long journey across the desert without eating. Camels can survive for several days without food.

A camel's heavy eyelids and long eyelashes protect its eyes from sand blown by desert winds. Its nostrils can close to prevent sand from going up its nose. And its thick lips allow it to eat even the prickliest desert plants without hurting itself.

Webbed toes and thick pads on the soles of a camel's feet make it easy for the animal to walk on the soft sand.

# MARINE TURTLES

Marine turtles live in warm seas and spend most of their time in the water. They look similar to land turtles, but marine turtles have much larger flippers to help them swim.

The flat shape of a marine turtle's shell helps it glide easily through the water.

Every year, female turtles haul themselves out of the sea and on to beaches at night to lay their eggs. Each female always returns to the same beach.

All the eggs hatch at the same time. The baby turtles hurry into the sea as fast as they can.

# CUTTLEFISH AND OCTOPUS

Cuttlefish are among the more colorful of all sea creatures. They are able to change the patterns on their brightly colored skin very quickly to help them hide from enemies. Their two large eyes help them see clearly underwater.

If an octopus is in danger, it squirts a cloud of inky liquid into the water in front of its enemy. Because the enemy is unable to see, the octopus escapes.

The octopus has eight arms. Underneath each of these arms are two rows of suckers. The octopus uses these suckers to cling tightly to rocks or to pull itself along. They are also useful for catching food.

# ZEBRAS AND GIRAFFES

Zebras and giraffes live in Africa. They both live in large groups called herds. Staying close together helps keep them safe from attack by fierce animals, such as lions.

These little birds are called oxpickers. They pick insects off a giraffe's skin.

Every zebra has its own special pattern of stripes. Sometimes tiny insects land on a zebra's back and make it itch. Zebras nibble each other's backs to get rid of the insects.

A giraffe uses its long tongue to gather leaves from the treetops. Its lips are protected from the sharp thorns by long hairs.

Giraffes find it very difficult to bend down because of their long front legs.

Grass is a zebra's favorite food, but sometimes it will eat leaves or tree bark.

Sometimes a roll in the dust gets rid of an itch.

# PENGUINS

Penguins are sea birds. They spend most of their lives in the water. They return to land only to lay their eggs and raise their chicks. Most penguins live in large groups called colonies.

Penguins slide across the ice on their chests. They use their feet and flippers to push themselves along.

As well as diving from the land into the sea, penguins are also able to leap from the sea onto the land.

Penguins cannot fly. Instead they use their wings to help them swim and dive.

All penguins store food inside their bodies in special pouches called crops. They use this food to feed their chicks.

Emperor and Adelie penguins are found in Antarctica. The Emperor is the biggest of all penguins.

Every year, each female Emperor lays one egg. The males then look after the eggs all through the winter until the chicks are ready to be born.

Each male holds his egg on top of his feet, tucked safely under a fold of feathery skin. When the egg hatches, the male looks after the chick for the first day or two. Then the female returns to help.

# ANIMAL QUIZ

Have fun trying to solve these puzzles.
You can discover all the answers by
looking through the book. If you get
stuck, look at page 48.

## BABY ANIMALS

Choose the correct name for each baby animal:     Pup     Chick     Calf     Cub

1

penguin

2

lion

3

seal

4

walrus

## WHO ARE THEY?

Can you remember what these animals are called?

1

2

3

4

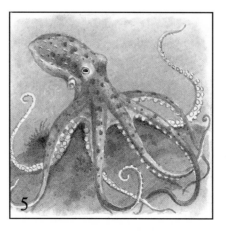

5

6

46

# FEEDING TIME

What is the favorite food of each animal below?

monkey

panda

zebra

koala

grass

eucalyptus leaves

fruit and nuts

bamboo

# WHERE DO THEY LIVE?

Where do these animals live?

camel

crocodile

parrot

zebra

seal

South American
rain forest

sea

desert

river

African
grasslands

# QUIZ ANSWERS

## BABY ANIMALS

The baby penguin is called a chick.
The baby lion is called a cub.
The baby seal is called a pup.
The baby walrus is called a calf.

## WHO ARE THEY?

Picture 1 is a cheetah.
Picture 2 is a toucan.
Picture 3 is a chimpanzee.
Picture 4 is an ostrich.
Picture 5 is an octopus.
Picture 6 is a polar bear.

## FEEDING TIME

The monkey likes to eat fruit and nuts.
The panda likes to eat bamboo.
The zebra likes to eat grass.
The koala likes to eat eucalyptus leaves.

## WHERE DO THEY LIVE?

The camel lives in the desert.
The crocodile lives in the river.
The parrot lives in the South American rain forest.
The zebra lives on the African grasslands.
The seal lives in the sea.

GREENLAND

Alaska

Canada

NORTH
AMERICA

U.S.A.

ATLANTIC OCEAN

PACIFIC OCEAN

SOUTH
AMERICA

AUSTRALIA

New
Zealand